This Little Tiger Book Belongs To:

To our little Petely boy

LITTLE TIGER PRESS
1 The Coda Centre, 189 Munster Road,
London SW6 6AW
www.littletigerpress.com
This paperback edition published 2002
First published in Great Britain 2002
Text and Illustrations © Catherine Walters 2002
Catherine Walters has asserted her rights to be
identified as the author and illustrator of this work
under the Copyright, Designs and Patents Act, 1988
Printed in Belgium
All rights reserved • ISBN 1 85430 768 1
2 4 6 8 10 9 7 5 3

Play Gently, Alfie Bear!

CATHERINE
WALTERS

LITTLE TIGER PRESS
London

"Can I play with the babies, Mum?" asked Alfie. He reached out to stroke his baby brother and sister.

"Only if you're gentle," said Mother Bear. "Remember, they are very small."

"Oh," said Alfie, disappointed. "Can't I play rough-and-tumble?"

"No, you can't."

"Or tug-of-war?"

"No, Alfie," said Mother Bear firmly . . .

"Why don't you find something to show them?" said Mother Bear. "The whole world is new to them out there."
Alfie looked puzzled.
"But I don't know what they'd like," he said.

The sounds of a fresh spring morning drifted into the cave.
"Bring them something that will soothe them," Mother Bear suggested. "Like the swishing of rain in the long grass or the rustle of young leaves on the trees."

Alfie set out. There were some big
black clouds in the sky, and he heard
a distant rumble from over the hills.
It gave Alfie an idea. It was much
better than the sound of rain swishing
in the grass, and better even than the
rustle of leaves. He couldn't wait to get
back to the babies.

Alfie raced into the cave. "Listen to this!" he shouted, and he banged two stones together as hard as he could. BANG! BANG! BANG! "Listen, I've brought you the sound of thunder!"

"No, Alfie," said Mother Bear. "That's far too noisy for the babies."
"Well, I think they liked it," mumbled Alfie.

Mother Bear chewed thoughtfully on a piece of hay. "Why not find the babies something sweet to eat, like a drop of dark winter honey, or a fresh shoot of grass," she said.

Alfie set out again. He walked on and
on until he reached the shores of the
lake. Then he stopped. He had an
even better idea than Mother Bear's.
"The babies will love it!" he cried, as
he paddled in the lake.

It was a long time before Alfie came
home again.
"Look, babies, I've got something
for you to eat," he called.

"You can't give them that," said Mother Bear,
taking a huge fish from Alfie's arms.
"It's bigger than they are!"
"But it took me ages to catch," protested Alfie.

Mother Bear stretched. A cobweb on the ceiling tickled her ear. "Of course," she said, "you could find something for the babies to feel, like the soft touch of the spring breeze or the tickle of a feather."

So Alfie went outside again. As he strolled through the trees, another thought came to him . . .

"Tickle, tickle, tickle," laughed
Alfie as he rushed back
into the cave.
"Aitchoo! Aitchoo!"
went the babies.

"You mustn't shake that stick at them," cried
Mother Bear, whisking it from Alfie's paws.
"The catkins have made them sneeze."
Alfie began to cry.
"You don't like any of my ideas," he sobbed.

The sweet scents of spring swept into the cave.
"Cheer up, Alfie," said Mother Bear.
"Maybe the babies would like to smell something sweet, like the scent of early flowers or a pine cone from the forest."

Alfie left the cave once again.
"I'll pick those flowers, just as Mother
Bear suggested," he thought.
But as he bent down to pick the first
flower, he saw something much more
interesting peeping through the grass . . .

Even before Alfie got inside the cave, Mother Bear stopped him. "Alfie, what are you doing?" she cried. "That's a skunk! They really stink. Take it back to where you found it, at once!"
So, Alfie let the skunk go. "I can't do anything right," he wailed. "I don't want to play with those silly babies, anyway. They're boring!"

It was starting to rain, but
Alfie didn't care. He sat on
a rock in front of the cave
and got wetter and wetter.

Mother Bear came
outside and wrapped
Alfie in a big bear hug.
"I'm sorry, Alfie," she
said. "I know you were
only trying to help."

Just at that moment, the sun came out,
and the rain sparkled in the light.
"Mother Bear!" shouted Alfie. "I've
seen something really special
for the babies to look at."

"Look, babies, a rainbow!" said Mother Bear, carrying them outside. The rainbow arched across the whole valley. But the babies seemed to be interested in something else. "They're staring at me, not the rainbow," said Alfie.

"Well, they must know what they like the best," said Mother Bear, giving all three of her cubs an enormous hug.